A promise is a promise

Dr. Tabatha M. W. Spurlock

Published by Parker & Co. Press, LLC
P.O. Box 50040
Richmond, VA 23250

Library of Congress Control Number: 2020916714

ISBN: (paperback): 978-1-952733-10-9
ISBN: (hard cover): 978-1-952733-09-3
ISBN: (e-book): 978-1-952733-11-6

Dedication

To my first born...Miss Kennedi Alyse!

You are the best gift ever from God. I want you to know how much I love and adore you. Some days I look at you, shake my head, and just smile. You are definitely a miniature version of me. It's admirable and scary at the same time. You have a big heart and you genuinely care for others. I thank you for being my rock and inspiration throughout my recovery. I couldn't have made it without you. I want you to know that your mommy will ALWAYS love you and have your back!

Kennedi was so excited about her upcoming family trip that she checked the calendar a million times. Each day, she was just a tad bit closer.

Her parents had promised her a dream vacation to her favorite place in the whole wide world! In her family, they never broke a promise until Mom came home from work with a brace around her leg.

"MOM! What happened?"
Kennedi yelled.

"I was in an accident today. My
leg is broken."

Kennedi immediately ran to her mom to give her a big hug.

"Mommy, are you going to be okay?" Kennedi cried out.

As tears rolled down her mother's face, she replied:

"Yes, Kennedi, I'm going to be okay. I feel better now that you're home. I do have some bad news, though."

"We know we promised but we will not be able to go to Princess Fairyland this year."

Kennedi pleaded, "But Mom, I really wanted to go. You and Dad PROMISED!"

"I'm sorry, Kennedi. It will take two months for me to be out of my wheelchair. As soon as I can walk again, we will pick back up with our planning."

"What if I push you through the park in your wheelchair? Yeah, it'll be lots of fun. I really want to go, and I also told my friends I was going," Kennedi said.

"I know you are excited about going and I'm very sorry.
I'm sure your friends will understand. It's not your fault.
Life happens..."

Kennedi laid down on her bed and began to cry. "I really wanted to go to Princess Fairyland to see the princesses!" Kennedi shouted.

Kennedi decided to create a Princess Fairyland vision board. Over the next few months, she made a list of all of the princesses and characters she wanted to see when her dream vacation would happen. She wanted to keep her dream alive.

"Kennedi, guess whaaaat?"
Her mom said with excitement.

Kennedi replied, "What, Mom?".

Her mom yelled, "WE'RE GOING TO
PRINCESS FAIRYLAND!"
Kennedi thought about it for a
second.
"Mom, are you sure this time? You promise?"
Her mom yelled, "YES, I PROMISE!"

Kennedi began to jump up and down. She ran around the room screaming, "YES, WE'RE GOING TO PRINCESS FAIRYLAND! WE'RE GOING TO FAIRYLAND!".

She grabbed her calendar, marked the new date, and began to tell her mom about the ideas she found online.

Kennedi was so happy and excited that she played dress-up every day with the princess costumes in her closet until it was time for the family trip!

TODAY IS THE DAY! They're heading to Princess Fairyland!

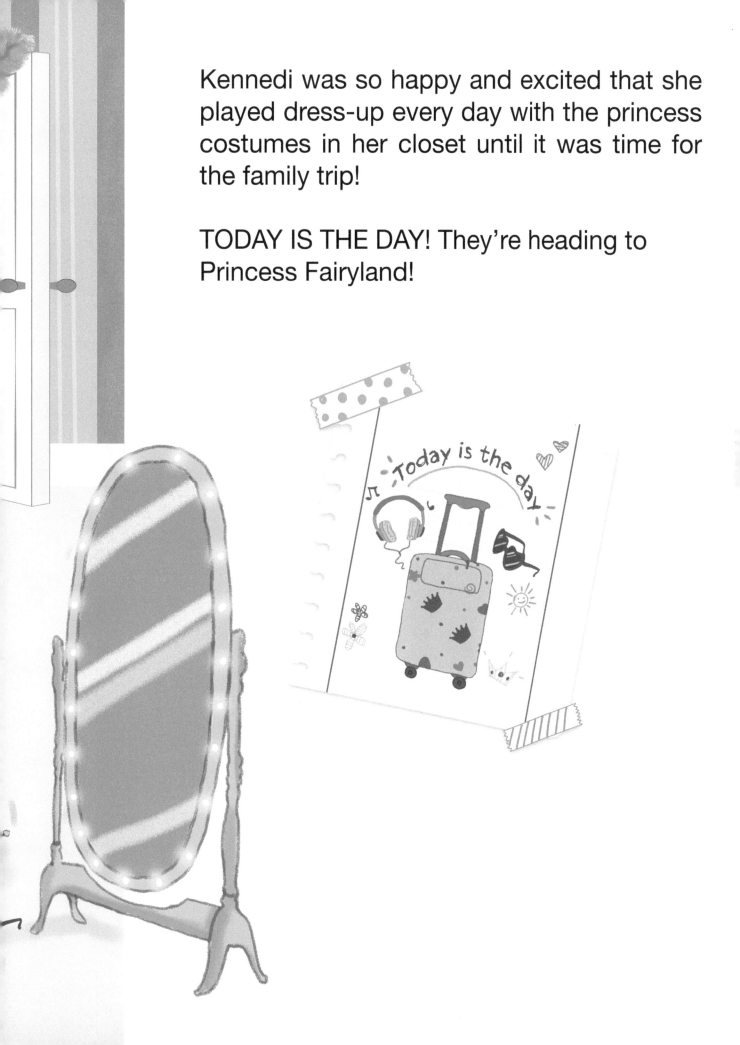

Today is the day

fairyland
here
we
come!

say cheese

♡♥ airport ♥♡

airport ☑
lunch with
princesses ☐

between clouds

smiles

love

They landed safely, hopped in an Uber, and shortly arrived at their five-star resort. Kennedi felt like she was on top of the world when she saw the huge pool with a slide. She could even order room service all day if she wanted!

perfect day!
FAIRYLAND
DAD
MOM
love mom & dad
CRAYON
CRAYON
CRAYON
love

Her family changed clothes to wear pink and black, Princess Fairyland designed t-shirts that said, "Mom," "Dad," and "Kennedi." And they were off to the park!

Greeted by a photographer upon arrival, they had a family picture taken in front of the Princess Fairyland sign.

happy

So much fun !!

Kennedi's mom then handed out wristbands to each of them for entry onto the rides.

"OH, WOW!" Kennedi yelled with excitement. "Princess Lina... Princess Mireya... Princess Sariya... This is so awesome!"

Kennedi skipped through the park in awe as she noticed each character. She ran up to each one to give them a big hug.

"Kennedi, come with me," her mom said. Kennedi had a puzzled look on her face as they walked into a castle. "SURPRISE!" Her mom shouted.

They received a warm, friendly greeting as their reservation was confirmed at check-in for their fairytale dining experience at the Fairyland Magic Table.

For the next two hours, Kennedi took pictures with princesses and enjoyed a magical dining experience as they sat next to stained-glass windows overlooking the park.

Kennedi hugged and chatted with every princess who visited their table. Her mom took plenty of pictures and videos so she would remember that day for the rest of her life.

The night was coming to an end, and it was time for her family to Uber back to the resort. Kennedi looked at her mom and said, "Mom, I had the BEST time of my life! Thank you for my dream vacation!" Her mom replied, "You're welcome, Kennedi. I'm glad you had a great time. Remember, a promise is a promise!"

The End

Certified Life Coach and Amazon Bestselling Author of "It Takes Money Honey - Freedom, Faith & Finances" Dr. Tabatha M. W. Spurlock holds a doctorate degree in Educational Leadership and Technology from the University of Phoenix. In her spare time, she enjoys dancing and spending quality time with family and friends. A fun fact about her is that she is bilingual.
She resides in Glen Allen, Virginia with her family.

CPSIA information can be obtained
at www.ICGtesting.com
Printed in the USA
LVHW072100250920
666878LV00021B/25